THE RAILWAY COMPUTER

THE RAILWAY COMPUTER

by

JEAN WILLS

Illustrated by Valerie Littlewood

HAMISH HAMILTON

LONDON

First published in Great Britain 1983 by
Hamish Hamilton Children's Books
Garden House 57–59 Long Acre London WC2E 9JZ

British Library Cataloguing in Publication Data
Wills, Jean
    The railway computer.—(Antelope books)
    I. Title   II. Littlewood, Valerie
    823'.914[J]   PZ7

ISBN 0-241-11007 6

Filmset in 'Monophoto' Baskerville by
Eta Services (Typesetters) Ltd, Beccles, Suffolk
Printed in Great Britain by Cambridge University Press,
Cambridge, England

Contents

Chapter 1
Cousins and Computers

THE COACH PULLED into a big bus station. "We'll take a twenty minute break," said the driver.

The thermometer outside the café read 30°C. "I could do with a cup of tea," said Mum. Tea, thought Alex! The café had sold out of ice lollies and cans. Alex had to make do with orange squash. But at least there was Space Invaders.

"I don't know what you see in those games." Mum eased her shoes off under the café table. Alex's school was getting a computer next term. He couldn't wait. He almost wished the

long summer holiday was over and done with already. Especially the next bit. Two weeks with his idiot cousins. How would he ever survive? He put another coin in the slot. "Wasting your money," grumbled Mum. "You should save it for Auntie Val's."

Mum had made him put half his pocket money aside for some weeks now. But the thought of the big fat lump he had to spend gave him no comfort. It seemed unlikely that Space Invaders, Pirates of Doom or Menace from Mars would have reached . . . what was the place called? Something to do with breakfast. Porridge? No, *Borage*. What a name!

"We'd better go." Mum was trying to get her shoes back on. The coach driver sounded his horn. Mum had to carry the shoes. She looked funny without her high heels. "How far to Borage?" she puffed, bright pink from running in the heat.

"Sixty miles odd," said the driver. "An hour and a half, if you're lucky and the engine doesn't boil."

Alex sat down again on his hot seat. The thick material behind his back

made his shirt stick wetly. He leaned forward, looking out at the empty yellow fields, pale sky. They passed a huddle of cows shaded by a wilted tree. An hour and a half. And at the end of it, Lena and Carl.

Last time he'd seen his cousins had been Christmas in their previous house. A short visit that, because

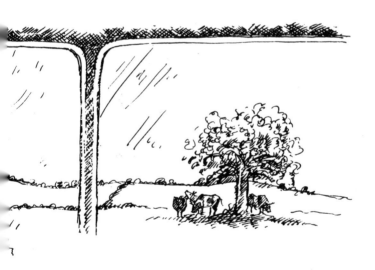

Mum couldn't stand Uncle Dick, and vice versa. Now Uncle Dick, who was a plumber, had gone away on a big building job. Auntie Val never visited *them* because Mum and Alex only lived in two rooms, and Auntie Val liked space. Not the Space Invaders sort, just room to spread herself.

"I wonder what it's like," Mum had her shoes perched on her lap. She'd wiped off the dust and was smiling at them.

"What?" said Alex.

"The new place, of course. Long garden, she said, with trains puffing up and down at the bottom."

"Trains don't puff," said Alex. "Not nowadays."

"Well, that's what she said."

There'd been Lena's letter too. Alex still had it in his pocket. 'Our new place,' Lena had written in her crazy writing, 'is pretty boring. Carl is boring too, like he always is when we change house. You know, throwing things.' Alex did know. He hoped Carl would have stopped by the time he got there. 'He even throws things at the train.'

"If there's a train why couldn't we have come on it?" Alex put Lena's letter back in his pocket underneath his calculator. "It would have been faster than this coach. And cooler. We could have opened all the windows."

"I did ask, but the man at the station told me trains don't run on that line any more."

Somebody was loopy, thought Alex, and he knew it wasn't him. He put his pocket calculator into his lap

13

and went off into a doze. When he came to again he was being chased round the galaxy by the Planet Aurora Space Fleet. Missiles were hurtling in all directions. All he had to do was press the button under his finger and . . . The coach gave a lurch. He opened his eyes.

CHANCE. They were just coming into a little dried-up village. The coach slowed into a bend, and there was a railway station with old-fashioned posters on the walls outside. COME AND VISIT THE SEASIDE. BOVRIL. PEAR'S SOAP. A signal box with a man looking out. They'd got caught in a time warp, thought Alex. Wouldn't Mum have a fit when she stepped off the coach and found herself in the last century? *In those shoes?*

"Borage next stop," called the driver.

They were running out of country, the fields growing smaller. The coach passed a dried river bed with a mere trickle of wetness down its middle. A lot of greenhouses, the sun glinting off them like silver splinters. Next a very big building. BORAGE FROZEN FOODS. They were still in the present all right. Then, suddenly, round a bend, was a proper road. Houses each side. Shops. Hot empty pavements and people in groups in the shade. Then the coach pulled up.

"There they are." Mum waved with her shoes through the window. Alex looked down at three hot faces. Auntie Val's, Lena's and Carl's.

Alex lifted the carrier bags off the rack. The big suitcase was in the boot.

16

As they waited for the driver to get it out Carl chased Lena round and round Alex. Then Carl fell over and began bawling. Lena, who'd been given Mum's shoes to carry, put them on and looked at herself sideways in a shop window. Mum left the carrier bags to Alex, while she and Auntie Val took turns with the suitcase. It was all much the same as ever, only in a different place.

When they reached the railway station Alex stopped. Lena came dancing back, like a pink grasshopper in her shorts and Mum's shoes. "Why is there a station and no trains?" asked Alex.

"There is a train," said Lena. "I told you in my letter." Alex saw a time-table by the station door. It was dated this year, but the trains only

seemed to run on Sundays. "I've been on it."

"Where to?"

"Chance. That's as far as it goes. Four miles to Chance, and back. Deadly boring." She fell over.

"You'll break your neck," said Alex. But Lena had picked herself up and was running on again.

He followed her along a road of little brick houses. Then left past a garden overgrown with brambles. They went in the front door. There was the same old furniture in different places. The big colour telly, which never worked properly. Through an untidy kitchen and out of the door was a garden like a long thin field. Grass gone yellow, crackling as he walked over it. "This is the prairie," said Lena. Down at the bottom grey

dried bushes and a pile of empty
polythene containers made a bit of
shade. On the other side of the fence
was the railway.

Clambering over, Alex was about
to slither down to the track when he
heard voices. Creeping along to the
next door fence, he listened. "What
we could do with," said a girl, "is
some sort of sideshow."

"How about George?" said a boy. "I wasn't thinking of a computer."

"Well, why not? All we would need is the right sort of software."

George? *A computer?* SOFT-WARE? Alex found a hole in the fence and peered through.

Chapter 2
Sunday Trains

THE FIRST THING Alex saw when he woke next morning was a computer. It was floating just above his head. Glistening keyboard. Video screen . . . He blinked and looked round the bedroom he shared with Lena and Carl. The other two were asleep. It was still very early, the sky outside pale yellow. Hot. He'd slept with only a sheet over him and had kicked that off. He crept to the window and looked out.

"What are you doing?" came Lena's sleepy voice.

"What does it look like?"

"You don't have to be so rude all the time," she hissed.

"Do you know those kids next door?"

"Why should I?" Lena went into the cupboard and when she came out she was dressed. If you could call replacing a nightdress with a bikini getting dressed.

"Those two," Alex began again. "They were down the end of their garden last night talking about a computer." Lena began posing in front of the mirror. Combing her hair. Making daft faces at herself. Carl woke up and began bouncing on his bed. Alex said, louder. "The boy said something about *software*."

"Not underwear?" Lena went into shrieks.

Downstairs Mum and Auntie Val

were doing their bird imitations again. It was always the same when they met. Chatter, chatter, chatter. After breakfast Alex escaped into the prairie. Lena followed him. "They do go yacketting on. They make my head ache."

"What about that software?" said Alex.

"You're as bad. Always asking daft questions."

"I bet you don't even know what software is."

"Yes I do. It's stuff you feed to computers."

Alex stared at her, then at the next door fence. "What do they do on Sundays?"

But Lena had lost interest. She went indoors and came back wearing Mum's shoes again. Plus beads like marbles, and a scarf of Auntie Val's. The scarf was so thin it was like looking through pink fog. Lena did a silly walk through the prairie, and Carl threw bits of dry earth at her.

Alex returned to the house. "I might get a job at that Nursery,"

Auntie Val was saying. "There's a nice lot of space there."

"They'll want somebody with green fingers," said Mum.

"And who says I haven't?"

Mum stood at the kitchen door. "You could try cutting that grass for a start."

Alex didn't see what space and green fingers had to do with babies. But then Mum's and Auntie Val's conversations never made much sense to him. Two weeks, minus one day. How would he ever survive it? Thirteen days! After he'd worked out the number of hours, minutes and seconds left on his pocket calculator he felt a bit better.

A door banged in the next house. Opening the front door quietly, he looked out. There were the kids he'd

28

seen through the hole in the fence before they'd gone off up their garden. Following them down the path was a man with a big toolbag, and a woman. Their Mum and Dad, he supposed. He let them all get well past, then gently pulled Auntie Val's front door shut behind him.

When he reached the gate they'd disappeared. He put on a spurt to the old station at the bottom of the road, but there was no sign of them in either of the two directions they could have gone from there. Left was a church. And it was Sunday morning. But men didn't go to church with no shirts on, carrying toolbags, did they?

He followed the road to the right – the one the coach had come in on, with the big bend at the bottom. All the shops were closed and the empty pavements were heating up already. Alex rounded the corner, passed BORAGE FROZEN FOODS, and there were the greenhouses he'd seen from the coach. BORAGE NURSERY. Outside in the shade of the greenhouses stretched rows of thirsty jaded plants. So that was the job Auntie Val had meant. Nothing to do with babies at all. But where were the people next door?

He turned back, and as he reached the place where the coach had stopped the previous day he heard banging. Metal on metal. Loud on a drowsy Sunday. He followed it to the station yard where cars were parked, and pushed open the station door. Inside was a small ticket office (closed), a shiny polished bench, a fireplace, doors marked LADIES

ROOM, PRIVATE, and an open one which led to the platform.

There were plenty of people here. Down on the line, and swarming all over a big engine on a siding. The boy from next door was there too, looking out of the signal box. People wore odd bits of uniform. A guard's hat was pushed up above a sticky forehead. Several wore railwaymen's trousers and no shirts. The station-master sweltered in his official jacket over baggy shorts. Alex saw the boy from next door carrying a kettle up into a carriage in the siding marked DINING CAR. What were they all doing? *Playing trains?*

He stopped by a poster and started to read it. THE OLD BORAGE STEAM RAILWAY. JOURNEY INTO THE PAST. EVERY

SUNDAY AFTERNOON. He'd been right, in a way. The Sunday train didn't go anywhere in particular. Just up to Chance, and back. The people here were enthusiasts. They'd rescued the bit of railway line between Borage and Chance after it had been closed down, together with a steam engine and four carriages, and put them all into working order.

Alex sat on the seat and watched them. They were mad. How could anybody want to spend hours messing about on an old railway, just to ride four miles up a track? Even Lena had said it was boring. He went to read the notice at the end of the platform. A little way past it the two lines crossed. That must be where the engine moved from the down line to the up. He went on to the track and began jumping the sleepers between the lines.

At the place where the lines crossed he climbed the bank. Over in the prairie Lena was still parading, but Carl had disappeared. Alex climbed the fence. As he jumped down he landed on a big round wooden disc, which wobbled slightly. Funny he hadn't noticed it the previous evening. He got on his knees to investigate.

"What are you doing?" Lena came running.

Alex had the disc off. He heaved it aside. "Be careful in those soppy shoes," he warned Lena. "There's a hole underneath big enough to fall in."

Lena knelt down. There were bricks round the hole. She picked up

a stone and dropped it in. Nothing for a moment, then a hollow splash. "It's a well!" said Lena. "Our own well. And we've discovered it!" Carl was bulldozing through the prairie towards them. "Cover it up, quick. I'm going up to tell Mum."

The rest of the day it was too hot to move. They talked and talked about the well. It was a change from the usual yacketty-yacking. "Nice that," said Auntie Val for the umpteenth time. "Our own water supply."

"We could put a bucket down and water this garden," said Mum. But Alex knew that even if it hadn't been for the heat nobody would bother.

He heard the steam engine come down the track and cross over. Later the family next door came home. After tea Alex climed the bottom fence. "Listen," he heard the boy say. "If we took George they could play Galactic Missiles, Saturn Invasion . . ." He stopped. Because this time Alex hadn't just peered through the hole. He'd climbed their fence and was sitting on the top, looking down at them.

Chapter 3
Ruby and George

"WHO ARE YOU?"

"Lena's cousin."

"Who's Lena?"

"My cousin."

"Ask a stupid question," said the girl. "Do you want to come over into our garden?"

"Yes please," said Alex, and jumped down.

"You're from next door, I suppose," said the boy.

Alex nodded. "I heard you talking through the fence. I wasn't spying on you or anything," he said hastily. "It's just . . . well, there's nothing for me to do here."

"Staying, are you?" said the boy.

"For a fortnight."

They exchanged names. The other two were Tess and Brian Barber. Brian was ten like Alex, and Tess was a year younger. "How old is Lena?" Tess went on to ask Alex.

"The same age as you."

"I didn't even know her name," said Tess. "She's not very friendly, is she?"

"She's not so bad," said Alex, surprised at himself. "They move about a lot, you see. She never gets time to settle anywhere before they're off again."

"You'd think she'd be good at making friends by now," said Tess.

"Not necessarily," said Brian. "If it was me I'd get fed up with new people all the time."

"Have you really got a computer?" said Alex. The other two looked at each other.

"How did you know George was a computer?" asked Brian.

Alex went red. "I listened to you last night," he admitted. But they didn't seem to mind. "Can you play Space Invaders?"

"You'd better come and see for yourself." Brian began leading the way up the garden. Tess ran ahead to a hutch under the lean-to, and brought out a white guinea pig with red eyes.

"This is Ruby. She's called that because of her eyes." Tess put the guinea pig down and it beetled into the wilting flowerbed to chew the bottom of an iris. The tall stalk tilted.

"Timber!" shouted Brian. He turned to Alex. "She's lethal." Tess made a grab for the guinea pig.

Mrs Barber came out of the kitchen door with a bowlful of washing-up water, which she emptied on the flowerbed. "Where did you spring from?" she asked Alex.

"Over the fence," said Brian. "Where's Dad?"

"Gone to bed. He's working night shifts next week."

"Alex is staying next door. Can I show him George?"

"As long as you don't switch on."

They went into the living room, and there was George. A real live computer, complete with keyboard, video and casette recorder. Fantastic!

"We can't use him now," said Brian. "George is an old computer,

you see. He hums and clicks quite a bit. Our Dad's a computer operator, and has to work long shifts at his job in the town. Night shifts are hardest. When he's working those he has to have extra sleep."

"Don't look so disappointed, Alex," said Tess. "Listen. Mum works part-time at the Nursery. Tomorrow we're going up there with her all day. But you can come in during the evening. Dad will have gone off to work by then.''

Brian grinned. ''And play Space Invaders until they're coming out of your ears.''

''Bring Lena too,'' added Tess.

Lena said she wouldn't go. All next morning she trailed about the prairie being an Egyptian belly dancer, with Auntie Val's pink fog scarf tucked in her bikini. ''She wouldn't like me.'' Lena paused in her belly dancing to nod at next door's fence. ''And I wouldn't like her,'' she hissed. ''She's a bossy sort of girl. You should hear her sometimes.''

''You don't have to whisper. There's nobody there, except Mr Barber and he's in bed.''

''Is he ill?''

''No.'' Alex explained about the

night shifts, and Brian and Tess going with Mrs Barber to the Nursery. "And Tess isn't bossy at all."

"You haven't heard her. If you think she's going to order me about the way she does poor Ruby. . . ."

"Have you seen Ruby?"

"Of course not. I don't want any friends, I told you."

"Ruby's a greedy guinea pig who eats everything. And she's called Ruby because of her eyes."

"Oh!" Lena flounced away. Then came back again. "There's no such thing as a guinea pig with red eyes."

"Yes, there is. If you'd got friendly with Tess instead of being so stand-offish you would have found that out for yourself."

"I don't care. I'm not going."

Mum and Auntie Val had gone

shopping, taking Carl with them. Lena went down to the well and Alex followed. "Let's take the cover off while Trouble's out of the way," said Lena. They peered into the cool murky hole. It was like putting your head into a refrigerator. Lena dropped a stone in.

"I've a lot of pocket money saved up," said Alex, after the splash.

"We could buy a bucket," said Lena.

Alex had been thinking more along the lines of ice lollies. Big expensive ones to butter Lena up, so she'd come with him next door. "Any old bucket would do for the well."

"Except we haven't got one. Only the pedal bin."

"What about *them*?" Alex pointed to the polythene containers.

"The last people left those behind."

"Well then . . . Don't tell me you haven't got a clothes line."

Lena nodded. "That's right. We haven't. Just a whirler." She nodded at the rotary drier at the top of the garden.

"No rope anywhere?" said Alex, but Lena shook her head. "Rope's very expensive."

"Please yourself." Lena began belly dancing again.

"Oh come on then. We'll go to the shops. I'm fed up with ice lollies anyway."

"That water will taste better than ice lollies," said Lena.

But it didn't. It was more like cough medicine, and a funny brownish colour. Getting one of the lightweight containers to fill up had been a job. It had floated on top of the water. They'd had to weight it down. And the plastic clothes line tied to its handle had made a big hole in Alex's money.

They hid the line under the containers as they heard Trouble returning. He looked extra hot and extra horrible. By evening he was throwing

things at everybody. But at least it made Lena change her mind about next door.

The funny thing was that as soon as they got together Tess and Lena began chattering like a pair of magpies. Just like Mum and Auntie Val, in fact. Brian nodded at Alex. "Let's go and feed George some software." Alex didn't need asking twice.

George's software was in cassettes. There were a lot more games like Space Invaders. Mysteries to solve. And puzzles too. At last Mrs Barber put her hand round the door. "I've made some lemonade."

As they moved loud voices started up outside. Alex went cold, then boiling hot. They've quarrelled, he thought. If Lena had been really awful Alex might not be allowed to come again . . .

Tess burst into the house. "Whatever is the matter?" said her mother.

"It's Ruby." Tess was almost crying. "She's eaten a hole right through the side of her hutch. She's gone!"

Chapter 4
Water

"IS THAT ALL?" said Brian.

"*All?*" Tess shrieked. "I might never see her again!"

They searched the garden for fallen flowerstalks to give them a clue, but the guinea pig had left no traces. "Even Ruby couldn't gnaw her way through this." Brian leaned against the big right-hand fence.

However they found several gaps beneath the other fence. "Ruby must have gone into our garden," said Lena. They climbed over and searched, but by bedtime there was still no sign of her.

Next morning Tess and Brian were looking again.

"Ruby hasn't come back?" asked Lena.

"No," sniffed Tess.

"Climb over to our side and we'll search our garden again."

Carl was in the middle of the prairie with a bowl of muddy water.

"That's a terrible waste of good water," Brian said. "Didn't you hear the news? Water's rationed."

"No watering gardens or washing cars," said Lena. "That's all."

"No it isn't. From today the water's being *cut off* between ten in the morning and four in the afternoon."

Alex looked at his watch. "Five minutes to go!" They raced indoors.

Mum and Auntie Val were just warming up for the day of talking ahead of them. "Stop it," said Lena. "And listen to us!" Out burst the news.

Auntie Val screamed. "Fill the bath. Fill everything!" Alex and Brian flew upstairs. The washbasin was full and the bath halfway up the sides when the water trickled off.

Downstairs the kitchen was covered in saucepans and pots. "What are we going to do with all this water?" said Lena.

"It'll disappear soon enough, don't you worry," said Auntie Val.

"We'll need a fair amount for the toilet," said Mum.

"You mean we can't pull the chain?" Lena was amazed.

"Each time you flush the toilet you use about 8 litres of water," said Brian.

Alex took out his pocket calculator. "That's roughly, say in one day . . . 240 litres for this house alone."

"The things they teach them nowadays," Auntie Val raised her eyebrows, then frowned at the calculator. "The things they have."

"You should see old George," said Brian. "Dad makes *him* work out our calculations."

"Poor old man," said Auntie Val.

"George is their computer, Mum!" said Lena.

Auntie Val looked at her sister, and

the pair of them looked nervously at the wall dividing the two houses. As though George was something out of an old James Bond film. Ticking over, dangerously. Detonation time . . .

"BANG!" Everyone jumped, but it was only Carl, fed up with his disgusting water, who'd decided to be a Space Cop instead. "I've shot you with my laser gun," he said to Brian. Then he shot everybody else and went upstairs.

After Auntie Val and Mum had gone off with the washing to see if the launderette was open, Lena remembered Carl. She flew upstairs, then called down to the others. Carl was somewhere in the bath, lost in a million bubbles. On the toilet stood Auntie Val's bottle of bath foam, empty.

Auntie Val and Mum were soon back. The launderette had been shut. Later on they all ate fish and chips in the shady part of the prairie. "You've got to eat," said Auntie Val as they picked the food over. But who wanted to eat, especially fish and chips, when the temperature had reached 30°C again? All anyone could think of was water. And the bath full of washing, next to the toilet wreathed in bubbles.

Next day they heard that the supply to some of the villages had been switched off altogether.

"At least we've got the well," said Alex.

"*That* awful water," said Lena.

"It would do to flush the toilet."

"If only it would rain," Lena started praying to the rain gods. Making a fine old hullabaloo.

"This awful heat!" Auntie Val moaned, flopping into a chair. She and Mum weren't talking so much now. The news they'd bottled up since Christmas had mostly escaped.

Mum turned on Alex. "Why don't you find something to do?"

Alex went and sat on the railway bank, while Carl threw earth over the fence at him. "I'll set the red-eyed monster on you," Alex threatened.

"You don't know where it is," said Carl.

"I wouldn't count on that," said Alex. Carl was quiet for a bit, then decided to retreat up the prairie. Alex slithered down and mooched along the track. Perhaps Ruby might have gone the same way, he thought.

When he reached the platform he found two men sitting on the seat

61

with their lunch boxes, talking earnestly. "Of course we'll have to cancel the train," said the man Alex recognised as the Sunday station-master.

"We can't do that, Jim," said the other man. "You know how close we are to having to shut down altogether for lack of money. We'd aimed to make this Sunday the biggest this summer. Sideshows. Stalls. Special teas in the Dining Car."

But the station-master went on shaking his head. "No water, no steam. No steam, no train."

"Look Jim, just supposing the weather turned . . ."

"What a hope! Well, we'll leave the decision until first thing tomorrow. No later mind."

Chapter 5
A Hard Slog

ALEX THOUGHT ABOUT the well. Surely *that* water would do for an old steam engine? He walked on past the signal box to the siding and into the engine shed. There was the big engine, PRINCE ALBERT. It was a handsome engine, green and shining in the mid-day sun. Not that Alex had ever bothered much about trains, except for the Underground at home. He climbed up into the cab, looking at all the dials and levers.

"What are you doing?" It was Brian, on his way home from the Nursery.

"Just looking," said Alex. "Where's the engine's tank, and how does the water get into it?"

Brian nodded to the little truck behind the engine. "This is the tender. The coal is kept in front and the water at the back. It's fed in from

the top." Brian turned, pointing towards the end of the siding. "That big tank on legs with the hose on the side is where the water is stored."

Alex jumped down and told Brian what he'd just overheard about the Sunday train. "That'll be old misery Jim Bates," said Brian. "Some enthusiast he is. We can't let him get away with cancelling this Sunday." They went and inspected the big water tank. It was almost empty.

"We've got a well," said Alex. "Come on, I'll show you." They walked back up the line and climbed over into Lena's garden. Alex heaved off the cover.

Brian's eyes opened wide. "Hot potatoes!" he said. "I'm going to tell Dad." But Mr Barber had gone off to work early. They would have to wait until he came home next morning.

Alex and Brian were out at the front gate first thing on Saturday morning. "You're quite sure?" said Mr Barber when they told him about the well.

Brian nodded. "We've asked Lena's Mum. She says we're welcome to any water that's there. We'll need a heavy bucket though."

"Take the one in the lean-to," Mr Barber rubbed his eyes. "I'll write a note for Jim Bates before I get to bed. You two can take it up to the station. Just make sure you catch him before he puts out a notice cancelling that train."

"Don't worry, Dad," said Brian. "We will."

The moment Jim Bates set foot in the station yard Brian and Alex pounced. He didn't want to know at first, but several other enthusiasts arrived, and *they* did. It wasn't long before they were all trooping up the line, climbing the fence into Lena's garden.

"I suppose we've just about enough water left to run Prince Albert down here," said Jim Bates after they'd hauled up a bucketful. "But if that well runs dry, don't blame me." He climbed back over the fence. "We'll fill up tonight then, ready for tomorrow."

Alex and Brian stayed there, practising with the bucket and clothes line until they'd got them operating really fast. "It's certainly thirsty work," said Brian. Auntie Val, Mum and Carl had gone shopping so they climbed the next door fence. Lena and

Tess were in the kitchen making shortbread for the Dining Car teas. "Phew!" said Brian. "It's worse than the inside of Prince Albert's boiler in here!"

"What about outside?" Lena pointed at the window. "Look!" Everything had gone hazy and the air smelt of bonfires. They ran down to the bottom of the garden. Up the line rolled . . . *smoke*!

Brian took off into the smoke with the others after him. It stung their eyes and made them cough. When they reached the platform they met Jim Bates staggering out of the station door with two big fire extinguishers. "Help me get these on to the dolly."

"But what's happened?" said Brian as they followed him to a funny sort of platform on wheels with a big lever in the middle.

"The grass has caught alight along the side of the cutting. We're still trying to put it out."

"What about the Fire Brigade?"

"They're away at a big forest fire. We'll have to cope with this ourselves."

"There's the water for Prince Albert . . ."

"There was," Jim Bates laughed grimly. The extinguishers were loaded on the dolly now. "You lads take the other side of that lever."

"What about us?" Tess nodded towards Lena.

"Go back and start filling those containers, both of you," said Brian.

71

"You'll need to fetch Dad's big funnel out of our lean-to."

"Come along now," shouted Jim Bates. "The whole cutting will be ablaze by the time we get there."

Working the dolly was a bit like moving a big bicycle, with a lever instead of pedals, and using hands not feet. When they reached the cutting they found several men stamping on the glowing grass, intent on prevent-

ing the fire spreading. "Here we are," called Jim Bates, and they ran forward for the extinguishers.

Brian nudged Alex and gave the dolly a push. Nobody noticed them go. One each side of the lever they worked their way back to the garden. Tess and Lena had begun filling the containers. Alex and Brian joined in. It was a hard slog. Bucket after bucket they hauled up, emptying the contents through the funnel into the containers and piling them on the dolly.

"Haven't we filled enough to take down the cutting?" puffed Lena. But just then the smoke thinned, and down the line somebody cheered.

"They must have beaten the fire after all," said Tess. "We've done all that work for nothing."

"No we haven't," said Brian. "Now we can use this water for Prince Albert."

They ferried it down to the engine on the dolly, while the girls worked on. Then they climbed up and emptied the water straight into Prince Albert's tank. "How much more water do we need to get the train to Chance and back?" groaned Tess, after the seventh run.

Brian shrugged. "Usually the pipe is just taken out when Prince Albert's tank spills over."

"Hadn't we better go and find out?" Alex nodded up the line.

"If we do," said Lena, "won't they stop us?"

"I know someone who won't," said Brian. "*George!*"

Brian raced indoors with the others

after him. The computer was plugged in and switched on. George hummed and buzzed and did his little click. Mrs Barber came hurrying in. "Your father's still asleep," she protested.

"I'm sure he won't mind if we wake him this time." Brian fed in a cassette and pressed some keys. The video came up with moving lines of information, and Brian pressed

another key to stop them. "There you are. Water. 2125 litres for a return trip."

"What is on that cassette?" asked Alex.

"A program Dad is setting up. Info about the railway. Handy, isn't it? Now if you can work out how many containers we need on your calculator . . ."

"I have," said Alex. "425."

"We'll never manage that number," wailed Lena.

"Listen," said Alex. "We've 25 containers, right?" The others nodded. "17 trips. And we've done 7 already."

"It seems like 70," moaned Lena.

"And we're not even halfway," added Tess.

"So come on!" Brian led the way

back to the well. And the hard slog began again.

Two trips later Mr Barber came out. Which was just as well because the enthusiasts up the line were finally returning. Jim Bates was wiping his black hands on his baggy shorts when Mr Barber and the children reached the engine shed. "Now I'll post that cancellation notice."

"Oh no you don't," said Mr Barber. "While you've been up the cutting these kids have begun watering Prince Albert. Now we'll help them finish the job. Then tomorrow we'll oil and fuel him, and he'll be all ready to go."

Chapter 6
Upline to Chance

ALEX AND LENA helped themselves to breakfast next morning before Mum and Auntie Val were up. Carl was a menace. "We can't leave him here alone," said Lena. So they had to haul him over the fence with them.

"Sorry," Lena said to Tess. "We couldn't leave Trouble behind."

But Tess smiled. "I think he's sweet," she said and gave him a piece of shortbread. Then she and Lena put the rest into tins while Brian and Alex and Mr Barber sorted out the video games they'd take to the station that afternoon.

During the morning it grew hotter and hotter. At mid-day they all went up to the station. Heat was shimmering off the line, and the platform burnt the soles of their feet. "I just hope enough passengers will turn up," Alex said as they walked home. "Supposing they don't even get here because of the heat?"

But he needn't have worried. As soon as they returned that afternoon a whole coach load of people arrived. Prince Albert puffed down to the points. Jim Bates, sweating in his station-master's uniform, stalked the platform before the waiting carriages. "Stand well clear of the edge there!" he bellowed.

Dark grey smoke belched from Prince Albert's funnel as he returned and the carriages were coupled on in front. The doors opened. People began climbing aboard. Even Mum and Auntie Val had turned up, to ride First Class. Alex hung out of the window wondering who'd look after George because Mr Barber was the guard. Then Mr Barber banged the last door shut, raised his green flag, blew his whistle, and climbed aboard the end carriage. The train moved off

and Alex looked into the waiting room. There was Jim Bates, the station-master, settling himself down to a game of Space Invaders.

Alex sat back in his corner as Prince Albert pushed them up the cutting. Its steep sides were black, and a burning smell still seemed to hang in the air. As they climbed out of the cutting, there was a tremendous view. Yellow fields, trees tinged with autumn too early. Villages crouched beneath the sky. A distant town. Not a glint of water anywhere.

"If this drought goes on," said Brian, "we might have to put that well into operation full-time."

"That must be where the monster's gone," said Carl. "Down the well." Tess looked mournful.

"If you can't be quiet," Lena said

to Carl, "you'll get put in First Class."

"What's that?" asked Carl.

"Where the baddies travel," said Alex.

Carl was interested. "I want to."

"You can't," said Brian. "You've only got a Third Class ticket."

Carl looked ready to bawl, but they were slowing down. "Already?" said Alex.

Brian looked at his watch. "Twelve

minutes. Bang on schedule. I just hope the water holds out."

"At least it's coasting most of the way back," said Tess.

At Chance some of the passengers went to explore the village. But most people waited in the shade for Prince Albert to take them back to Borage. There were stalls set all along the platform selling everything from wilting plants to old railway and computer magazines. Alex spent his remaining pocket money on the latter.

The journey back lasted ten minutes. Alex thought of the hard slog the day before. Getting all that water out of the well and on to the dolly, backwards and forwards to Prince Albert. And how they'd ached afterwards. Later, as they waved goodbye to the coach, Alex couldn't help remembering his own arrival in Borage, when he'd wondered how he would ever survive.

That night the sky grew not just black, but ebony. Giant forks of lightning played across it. Lena was scared, but Carl liked it. He liked it so much that he managed to slip out through the back door when nobody was looking. When he returned Auntie Val nearly had a fit. "A little drowned rat," she shrieked. But

whether she meant Carl or what he was holding Alex never discovered.

"What is it?" said Lena.

"The monster." Carl held up a struggling Ruby. "It's shrinked in the rain."

Next day Mr Barber fixed up Ruby's hutch with a chunk of old railway sleeper. "Let's see her get out of that," he said.

The second week of Alex's holiday turned out even better than the first. It rained most of the time, but who cared? There was water again. And so much to do. If it wasn't George, it was the railway. Or both. Lena and Tess were already cooking for next Sunday's Dining Car tea. And Carl . . . well, everybody had to admit that Carl and Ruby were made for each other.